Nobody Twinkles Like You

By Kerry Long

Illustrated by Susi Galloway

Shine Bright
♡
Kerry Long

Order this book online at www.trafford.com/07-1976
or email orders@trafford.com

Most Trafford titles are also available at major online book retailers.

Note for Librarians: A cataloguing record for this book is available from Library
and Archives Canada at www.collectionscanada.ca/amicus/index-e.html

Printed in Victoria, BC, Canada.

ISBN: 978-1-4251-4627-6

*We at Trafford believe that it is the responsibility of us all, as both individuals
and corporations, to make choices that are environmentally and socially sound.
You, in turn, are supporting this responsible conduct each time you purchase a
Trafford book, or make use of our publishing services. To find out how you are
helping, please visit www.trafford.com/responsiblepublishing.html*

*Our mission is to efficiently provide the world's finest, most comprehensive
book publishing service, enabling every author to experience success.
To find out how to publish your book, your way, and have it available
worldwide, visit us online at www.trafford.com/10510*

www.trafford.com

North America & international
toll-free: 1 888 232 4444 (USA & Canada)
phone: 250 383 6864 ♦ fax: 250 383 6804
email: info@trafford.com

The United Kingdom & Europe
phone: +44 (0)1865 722 113 ♦ local rate: 0845 230 9601
facsimile: +44 (0)1865 722 868 ♦ email: info.uk@trafford.com

10 9 8 7 6 5 4 3 2

Dedicated to...
All my little stars—
Taylor, my inspiration
Kasandra, my dancing spirit
Madison, my gentle heart

On a starry night in the Milky Way,
a curious little star sparkled.
Blinker is his name.

He peeked down through the clouds
to explore something new.

He zoomed in closer
and discovered a farm with
mother animals and
their babies too.

Blinker saw a mother cow and her baby calf.
The mother cow told the baby calf,
"I am so proud of you. You are going to be the best
dairy cow of them all.
You are so sweet and so strong.
You will grow really tall!"

Blinker saw a prize-winning pig.
She was tucking her two piglets into bed.
"I am so proud of you,"
the mother pig told her tiny pair."
"You will both win blue ribbons
at the county fair."

Blinker saw some ducks on a pond.
The mother duck swam with six ducklings in a row.
She told her ducklings,
"I am so proud of you.
Swim as fast as you can go.
Just follow me and I will teach
you what you need to know."

Then Blinker found a big barn.
He saw a mother horse with a baby colt lying on the hay.
The mother horse told her baby colt,
"I am so proud of you.
You will run wild and free one day."
She leaned over and said goodnight.
All of the animals had gone to sleep underneath the moonlight.

Blinker paused and sat down on a cloud with his head hung low.
He didn't know how to fit in with this world
or if he would ever grow.

Mother star came over to ask,
"What makes you cry?"
Blinker sighed and with sadness he replied, "I can't make milk.
I have never won first prize. I can't swim or run wild and free.
There isn't anything special about me."

Just then Blinker heard his brother Zap shout his name.
Oh no Zap's light was starting to fade!

Blinker rushed over to give him a charge.
Now Zap's light was no longer out.
It was shining quite large.

Mother star softly said,
"You see every star is different.
Every star has special things
they can do. Please do not
worry or try to change you.
Be magic and be bright.
You are a wish star for children
at night.
Oh my little star, you make
me very happy and proud too.
You have to believe that
nobody, nobody twinkles
like you."

Now Blinker realized we all shine
in our own way.
He hopped back into his spot in
the Milky Way and that is where he
twinkles still to this day.

Printed by
EDWARDS BROTHERS
www.edwardsbrothers.com
03SKC10MDJa